Shining Brass

Book 1, Grades 1–3

18 repertoire pieces and studies

For brass instruments

𝄞 **Brass**	Trumpet · B♭ Cornet · E♭ Soprano Cornet · Flugelhorn · E♭ Horn Horn · Trombone · Baritone · Euphonium · B♭ Bass · E♭ Bass
𝄢 **Brass**	Trombone · Baritone · Euphonium
𝄢 **E♭ Tuba**	E♭ Tuba

Composers

Tom Davoren, John Frith, Timothy Jackson, Peter Meechan,
Lucy Pankhurst, Philip Sparke and David A. Stowell

Project consultant

Nicky Daw

ABRSM

Recordings

This volume comes with a CD. This includes a single recorded performance of every piece (played variously by E♭ Horn, Horn, Trombone, Euphonium, or E♭ Tuba) as well as complete backing tracks recorded from the B♭, E♭ and F piano accompaniment books. Additionally, a full performance of every piece played on a B♭, E♭ and F instrument can be downloaded from www.abrsm.org/shiningbrass.

Next to each piece you'll find track numbers – ① – and the following icons:

🎵 (Trombone)   Performance track (the instrument playing on the CD is shown in brackets)

🎹 B♭   Backing track(s) (and applicability for B♭, E♭ or F instrument)

 Players can also download Speedshifter – a free practice tool from ABRSM that allows you to vary the speed of audio from CD or MP3 without altering the pitch. www.abrsm.org/speedshifter

First published in 2012 by ABRSM (Publishing) Ltd, a wholly owned subsidiary of ABRSM, 24 Portland Place, London W1B 1LU, United Kingdom

Reprinted in 2012

© 2012 by The Associated Board of the Royal Schools of Music
ISBN 978 1 84849 440 4
AB 3694

A CIP catalogue for this book is available from The British Library.

Cover design by www.adamhaystudio.com
Music origination by Andrew Jones
Printed in England by Caligraving Ltd, Thetford, Norfolk

Recording credits (including track numbers)
Played by Corinne Bailey (Horn) 4, 6, 8, 12, 15, 17; Jonathan Bates (E♭ Horn) 10, 14, 16; David Gordon-Shute (E♭ Tuba) 2, 11, 18; Amos Miller (Trombone) 1, 3, 7; Lewis Musson (Euphonium) 5, 9, 13; Harvey Davies (Piano) 9, 10, 13, 14, 16, 25–8, 30, 37–40, 42, 49–52, 54; Lindy Tennent-Brown (Piano) 1–4, 7, 8, 15, 19–24, 29, 31–6, 41, 43–8, 53

Recorded in October 2011 at All Saints' Church, East Finchley and in November 2011 at Carole Nash Recital Room, Royal Northern College of Music, Manchester
Produced by Sebastian Forbes
Co-produced by Nicky Daw
Balance Engineering by Ken Blair
Assistant Engineer Chris Daw
Audio Editing by Ken Blair
A BMP Production for ABRSM

With particular thanks to Alan Bullard for his contribution to this project.

Contents

			𝄞 Brass	𝄢 Brass	𝄢 E♭ Tuba
	A Knight's Tale	Philip Sparke	4	16	28
	Romanza	Tom Davoren	4	16	28
	Strollin'	David A. Stowell	5	17	29
	Waltz for E.	Tom Davoren	6	18	30
*	One, Two, Three!	Peter Meechan	6	18	30
*	Puppet's Dance	Philip Sparke	7	19	31
	A Walk in the Rain	David A. Stowell	7	19	31
	My Lady's Pavan	Philip Sparke	8	20	32
	Hangin' with Monti	Tom Davoren	8	20	32
	Tennessee Rag	Philip Sparke	9	21	33
*	Haunted House	Peter Meechan	10	22	34
*	High Street	David A. Stowell	10	22	34
	Rondo Olympia	Tom Davoren	11	23	35
	Sicilienne	Lucy Pankhurst	12	24	36
	Broken Dreams	John Frith	12	24	36
	Purple Shade	Peter Meechan	13	25	37
*	How's Tricks?	Timothy Jackson	14	26	38
*	Summer Sound	Peter Meechan	15	27	39

* Unaccompanied studies

Using Shining Brass

Instrument	Part	Piano accompaniment/ Backing track
Trumpet	𝄞 Brass	B♭
B♭ Cornet	𝄞 Brass	B♭
E♭ Soprano Cornet	𝄞 Brass	E♭
Flugelhorn	𝄞 Brass	B♭
E♭ Horn	𝄞 Brass	E♭
Horn	𝄞 Brass	F
Trombone	𝄞 Brass	B♭
	𝄢 Brass	B♭
Baritone	𝄞 Brass	B♭
	𝄢 Brass	B♭
Euphonium	𝄞 Brass	B♭
	𝄢 Brass	B♭
E♭ Bass	𝄞 Brass	E♭
E♭ Tuba	𝄢 E♭ Tuba	E♭
B♭ Bass	𝄞 Brass	B♭
B♭ Tuba *	𝄢 B♭ Tuba *	B♭
F and C Tubas †		

* A separate part for B♭ Tuba
is available for download at
www.abrsm.org/shiningbrass.

† For F and C Tubas, the
solo part may need to be
adapted or the solo part and
accompaniment transposed.

Brass

A Knight's Tale

G1 tuba

Philip Sparke

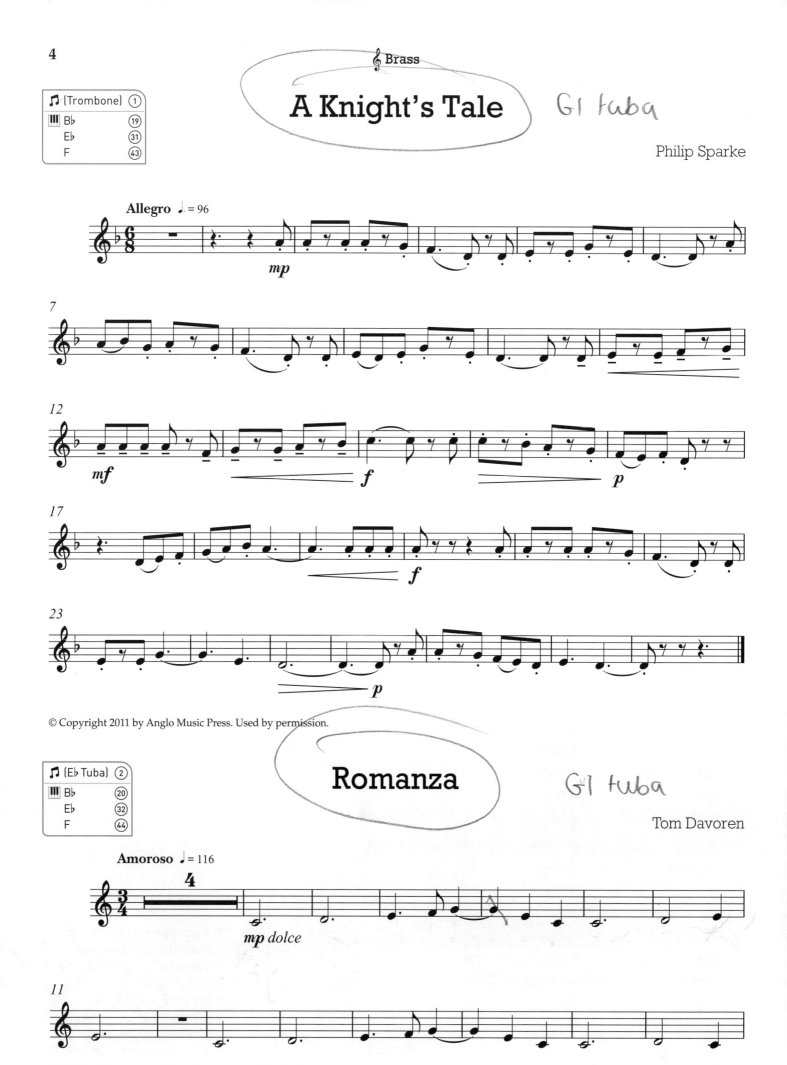

Romanza

G1 tuba

Tom Davoren

19

poco rit.

mf

29 **a tempo**

mp

p

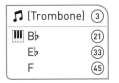

♫ (Trombone)	③
III Bb	㉑
Eb	㉝
F	㊺

Strollin'

Grade 1 (B)

David A. Stowell

Steady swing ♩ = 96

f

6

11

mf

f

16

6

 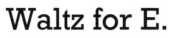

Brass

in memory of Esbjörn Svensson

Waltz for E. Tuba G1 (B)

Tom Davoren

1 © 2012 by The Associated Board of the Royal Schools of Music

One, Two, Three! Tuba G1 (C)

Peter Meechan

1 © 2012 by The Associated Board of the Royal Schools of Music

AB 3694

ϕ Brass

🎵 (Horn) ⑥

Puppet's Dance

Tuba G1 (C)

Philip Sparke

🎵 (Trombone) ⑦
🎹 B♭	㉓
E♭	㉟
F	㊼

A Walk in the Rain

G2 horn

David A. Stowell

8

G2-horn

♪ Brass

My Lady's Pavan

Philip Sparke

3

for Monti, the Beagle

Hangin' with Monti

Tom Davoren

Tennessee Rag

Philip Sparke

♪ Brass

Haunted House

Peter Meechan

High Street

David A. Stowell

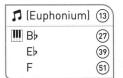

Rondo Olympia

Tom Davoren

🎼 Brass

Sicilienne

Lucy Pankhurst

Broken Dreams

John Frith

Purple Shade

Peter Meechan

♪ Brass

How's Tricks?

Timothy Jackson

♪ (Horn) ⑰

Summer Sound

Peter Meechan

A Knight's Tale

Philip Sparke

Romanza

Tom Davoren

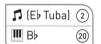

Strollin'

David A. Stowell

𝄢 Brass

in memory of Esbjörn Svensson

Waltz for E.

Tom Davoren

𝄞 (Euphonium) ⑤

One, Two, Three!

Peter Meechan

Puppet's Dance

Philip Sparke

A Walk in the Rain

David A. Stowell

My Lady's Pavan

Philip Sparke

for Monti, the Beagle

Hangin' with Monti

Tom Davoren

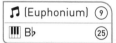

Tennessee Rag

Philip Sparke

Haunted House

Peter Meechan

🎵 (E♭ Tuba) ⑪

High Street

David A. Stowell

🎵 (Horn) ⑫

Rondo Olympia

Tom Davoren

𝄢 Brass

Sicilienne

Lucy Pankhurst

Broken Dreams

John Frith

Purple Shade

Peter Meechan

How's Tricks?

Timothy Jackson

♩ (Horn) ⑰

Summer Sound

Peter Meechan

A Knight's Tale

Philip Sparke

Romanza

Tom Davoren

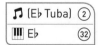

Strollin'

David A. Stowell

𝄢 E♭ Tuba

in memory of Esbjörn Svensson

Waltz for E.

Tom Davoren

🎵 (Horn) ④
🎹 E♭ ㉞

🎵 (Euphonium) ⑤

One, Two, Three!

Peter Meechan

Puppet's Dance

Philip Sparke

A Walk in the Rain

David A. Stowell

𝄢 E♭ Tuba

My Lady's Pavan

Philip Sparke

for Monti, the Beagle

Hangin' with Monti

Tom Davoren

Tennessee Rag

Philip Sparke

𝄢 E♭ Tuba

♫ (E♭ Tuba) ⑪

Haunted House

Peter Meechan

♫ (Horn) ⑫

High Street

David A. Stowell

Rondo Olympia

Tom Davoren

Sicilienne

Lucy Pankhurst

Broken Dreams

John Frith

Purple Shade

Peter Meechan

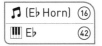

𝄢 E♭ Tuba

How's Tricks?

Timothy Jackson

(Horn) 17

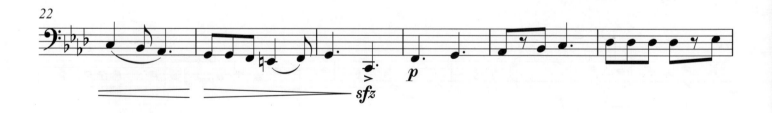

Summer Sound

Peter Meechan